Te quiero, carita sucia

Lisa McCourt

Ilustraciones de Cyd Moore

SCHOLASTIC INC.

New York   Toronto   London   Auckland   Sydney
Mexico City   New Delhi   Hong Kong   Buenos Aires

Para Aimee — L. M.
Para mis adorados
Lindsay y Branden — C. M.

Originally published in English as *I Love You, Stinky Face*

Translated by Mari Luz Ponce

ISBN 0-439-63931-X

Text copyright © 1997 by Lisa McCourt.
Illustrations copyright © 1997 by Cyd Moore.
Translation copyright © 2002 by Brosquil Ediciones, Avda. Equador, 101-12a, Valencia 46025, Spain.
All rights reserved. Published by Scholastic Inc. SCHOLASTIC and associated logos are trademarks and/or registered trademarks of Scholastic Inc.

12 11 10 9 8 7 6 5 4 3 2 1   4 5 6 7 8 9/0

Printed in the U.S.A.

First Scholastic Spanish printing, September 2004

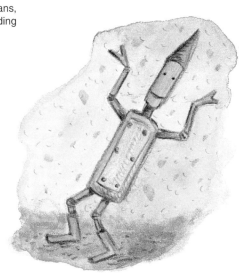

"Te quiero, mi pequeñín" —dijo mamá mientras me arropaba en la cama. Pero yo quería preguntarte algo.

Mamá, ¿qué pasaría si yo fuese un enorme y

terrorífico gorila? ¿Me querrías entonces, mamá?

"Si fueses un enorme y terrorífico gorila, te peinaría todo el cuerpo para asegurarme de que no tuvieses ningún enredo en el pelo".

feliz cumpleaños ... feliz

"Y te haría un pastel de cumpleaños de plátanos, y te diría TE QUIERO, MI GORILA GRANDULLÓN Y TERRORÍFICO".

Pero mamá, mamá, ¿qué pasaría si yo fuese una mofeta apestosa y oliese tan mal que todo el mundo me llamara...

CARA SUCIA?

"Entonces te daría
un baño y te frotaría
con jaboncito suave
y perfumado".

"Y si aún así todavía olieses mal, no me importaría, y te abrazaría muy fuerte para susurrarte en la oreja: TE QUIERO, CARITA SUCIA".

"Entonces te compraría un cepillo de dientes más grande para tus enormes colmillos y me aseguraría de que te los lavases cada noche para que estuviesen fuertes y sanos".

"Y si te doliese la garganta, metería la cabeza dentro de tu gran bocaza para estar segura de que te encontraras bien, y te diría TE QUIERO, MI FEROZ COCODRILO".

Pero mamá, mamá, ¿qué pasaría si yo fuese un terrible dinosaurio carnívoro, con las garras afiladísimas, y por las noches rompiera las sábanas a tiras mientras estuviese durmiendo?

"Entonces te daría
de comer mucha carne,
si te gustara tanto.
Y te cosería las
tiras de las sábanas
cada día, porque
seguro que las
habrías roto
sin querer".

"Y cada noche te arroparía con las sábanas recién remendadas, y te diría despacito TE QUIERO, MI DULCE Y TERRIBLE DINOSAURIO".

Pero mamá, mamá, ¿qué pasaría si yo fuese una criatura de los pantanos y tuviera el cuerpo envuelto en algas pegajosas y malolientes, y si no pudiese nunca dejar el pantano porque si no me moriría?

"Entonces construiría una casa al lado del pantano, y me quedaría contigo para cuidarte siempre. Y cuando salieses a la superficie te diría TE QUIERO, MI PEQUEÑO Y PEGAJOSO MONSTRUO DEL PANTANO".

Pero mamá, mamá, ¿qué pasaría si yo fuese un **alienígena verde** del planeta Marte, y comiese bichos en vez de chocolatinas?

"Entonces te vestiría con ropa de muchos colores para lucir tu preciosa piel verdosa...

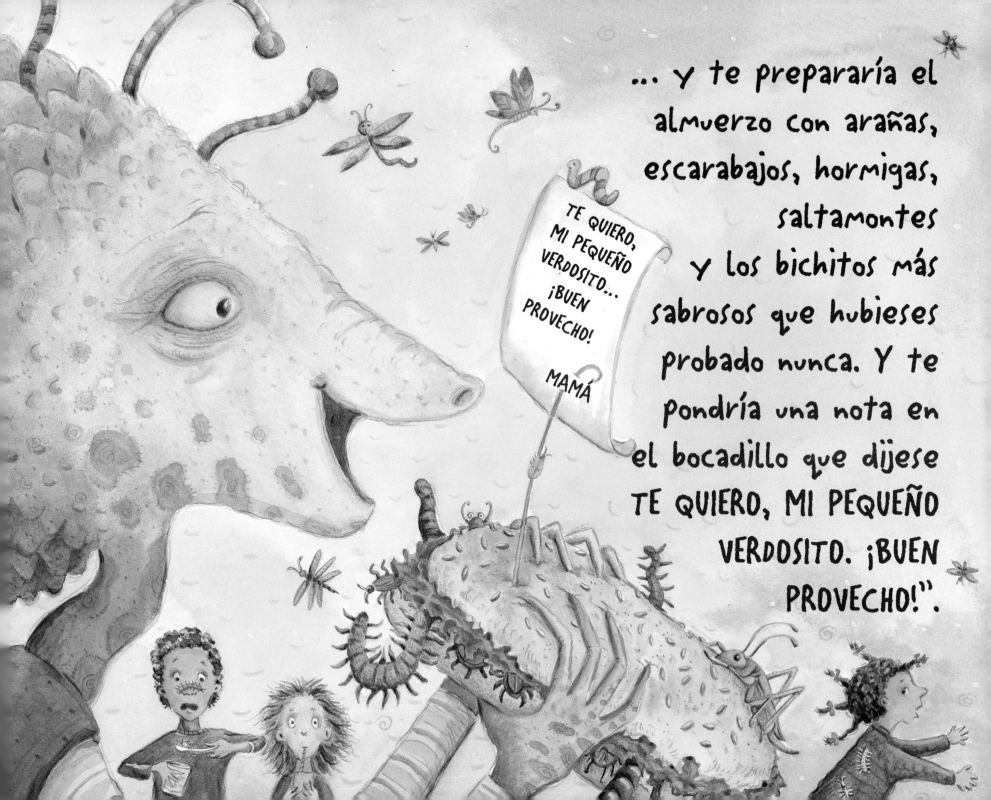

"Entonces te miraría directamente al enorme ojo y te diría TE QUIERO, MI PEQUEÑO CÍCLOPE, y te cantaría una nana mientras que tu párpado gigantesco se fuese entornando poquito a poquito hasta que se cerrase del todo y te quedaras dormido".

Te quiero, mamá.

"Yo también te quiero, mi cielo".

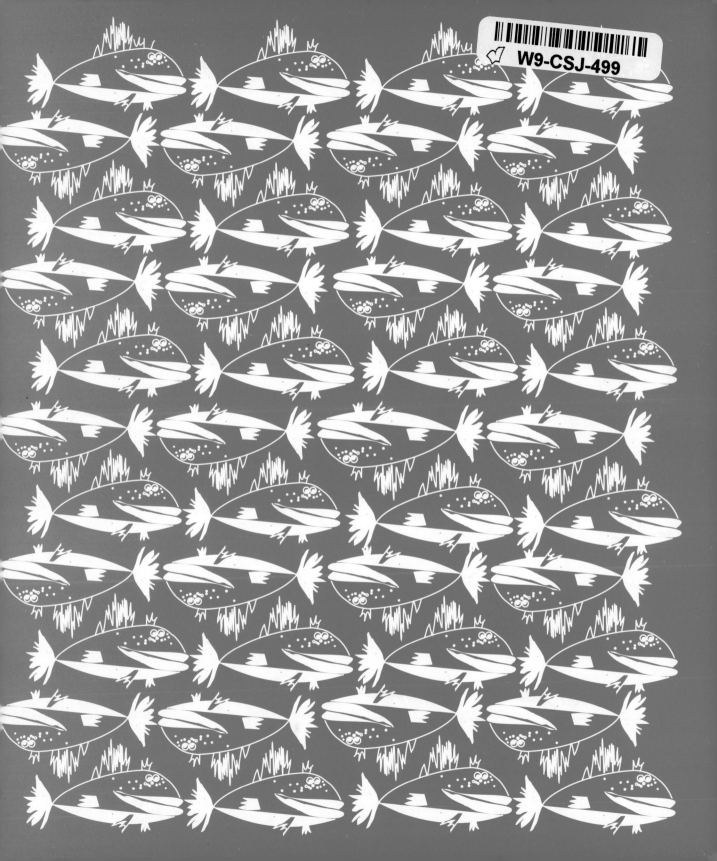

To those who believed in the book,
especially Terry, Barbara, and Jane.

And to my husband, Steve, who has
always believed in me.
M.W.

To my daughters, Lena
and Olga
A. S.

Book Design and Production by:
Art & International Productions
Jim Tilly & Sasha Sagan

Published by: Misty Mountain Press
P.O. Box 773042
Eagle River, Alaska 99577

First Printing January, 1993.
Second Printing, June, 1993.
Printing in Hong Kong

Library of Congress Catalog Card Number: 92-83704

ISBN 0-9635083-2-6

THE BIG

FISH
An Alaskan Fairy Tale

Written by Marcia Wakeland
with illustrations by Alexander Sagan

Misty Mountain Press
Eagle River, Alaska

Come, my friend, and listen to a wonderful, magical tale.
About a little girl named Lena who lived in a small river vale.
She loved to do so many things, but she had just one great wish;
It was her dream, a fantastic dream--she wanted to catch a big fish.

Lena lived in a big place called Alaska. A place where glaciers slide for miles down giant stone mountains. Cabbages grow so big that it takes two people to lift them. Caribou run in herds that cover miles of endless tundra. And big, big fish swim in deep, icy rivers. The fish are called King Salmon.

Lena had seen pictures of the great King Salmon. He could weigh as much as a baby moose. Lena was afraid of the big fish. She felt so small. But it was her dream to catch the King Salmon. She didn't know why.

Lena went to her father. "I want to catch a BIG fish," she said. "My little girl wants to catch a big fish?" he asked. Lena nodded. So he smiled and made her a strong pole from an alder branch with a thick line and a shiny hook.

She found her grandpa. "I want to catch a BIG fish," she said. "A BIG, BIG fish?" he asked. Lena nodded. So he gave her his secret bait--and a big hug. She put the secret bait on her strong pole. Then she cast her line into the stream and waited.

Of course,

she didn't want a small bite.

She didn't want a

medium-sized bite.

She wanted a

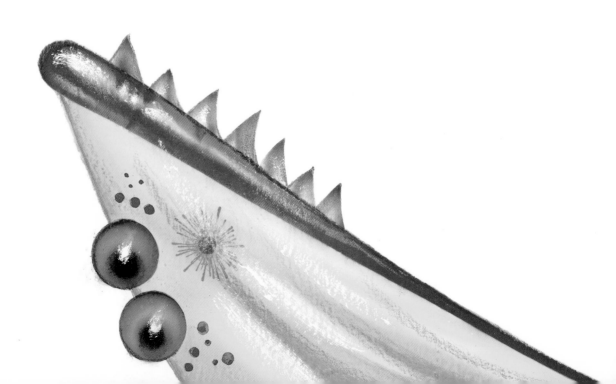

BIG

bite.

But.....she didn't get a bite at all.

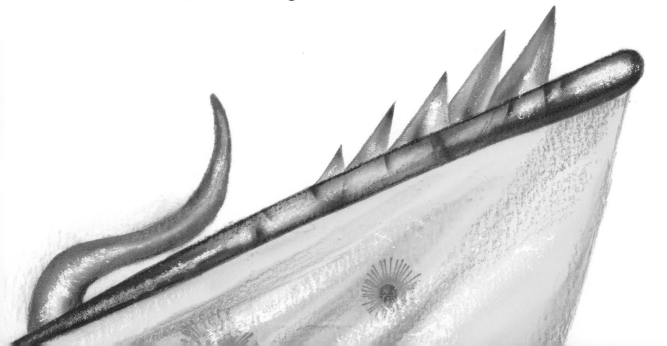

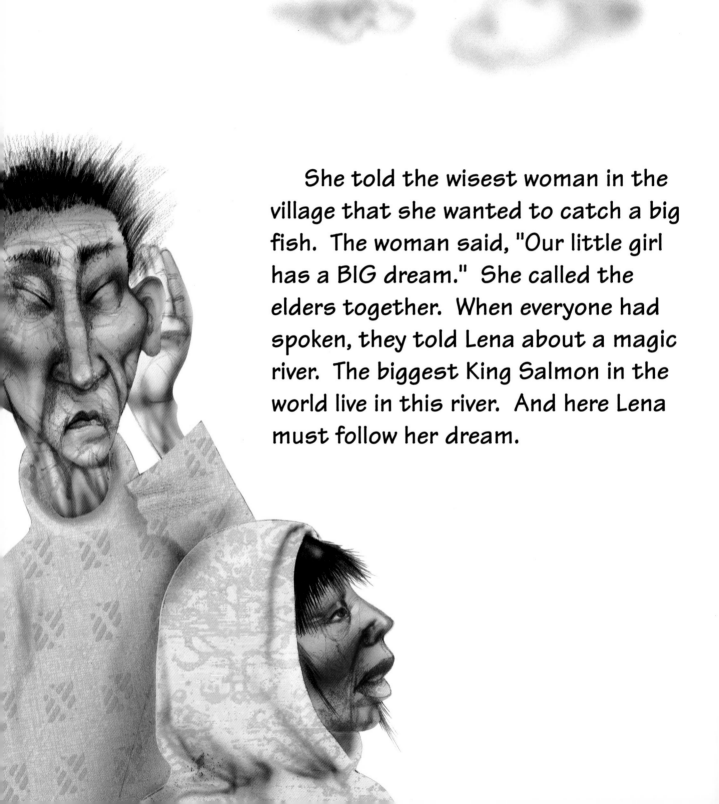

She told the wisest woman in the village that she wanted to catch a big fish. The woman said, "Our little girl has a BIG dream." She called the elders together. When everyone had spoken, they told Lena about a magic river. The biggest King Salmon in the world live in this river. And here Lena must follow her dream.

The wisest woman took Lena
on the long journey. Hours and
hours passed, until the midnight
sun had to chase away the
darkness. Then just as Lena
asked, "Are we there yet?",
they came to the
magic river.

It was like no river Lena had ever seen. It was so blue that she had to blink to be sure it was real. The water flowed deep and wide and rolled powerfully, majestically. The sunlight made the water shine and twinkle as if it were full of jewels--diamonds, sapphires and yes, even gold. This was a place fit for a king--King Salmon.

Lena shivered with excitement. Surely here she wouldn't get a tiny, small bite. Here she wouldn't get an average, medium-sized bite. Here she would get a BIG, BIG bite.

She cast her line, and she waited and waited and waited....but she STILL did not get any bite at all.

Big tears began to roll down Lena's cheeks like drops of rain. The wisest woman was watching. After a while she said, "Why are you crying, little one?"

"I will never catch the King Salmon. I'm just no good. Why did I ever have such a silly dream?" Lena sniffled. "I'm just a little girl, after all." But before she could say another word, she felt her pole bend in half, and she had to hold on with all her might.

"I have a bite! A BIG bite!" she squealed as she dug in her heels. "I have the King Salmon." She drew back hard on her pole, but she felt her feet slip a little. She drew back again, but before Lena could call for help, the big fish pulled her into the icy, deep waters of the magic river.

When she opened her eyes she was staring up at the biggest fish she could ever imagine. She saw his big mouth and his big teeth....and she began to shake. But when the big fish looked down at her, she saw that his eyes were kind. And when he began to speak, his voice was soft and gurgling, like water running over rocks.

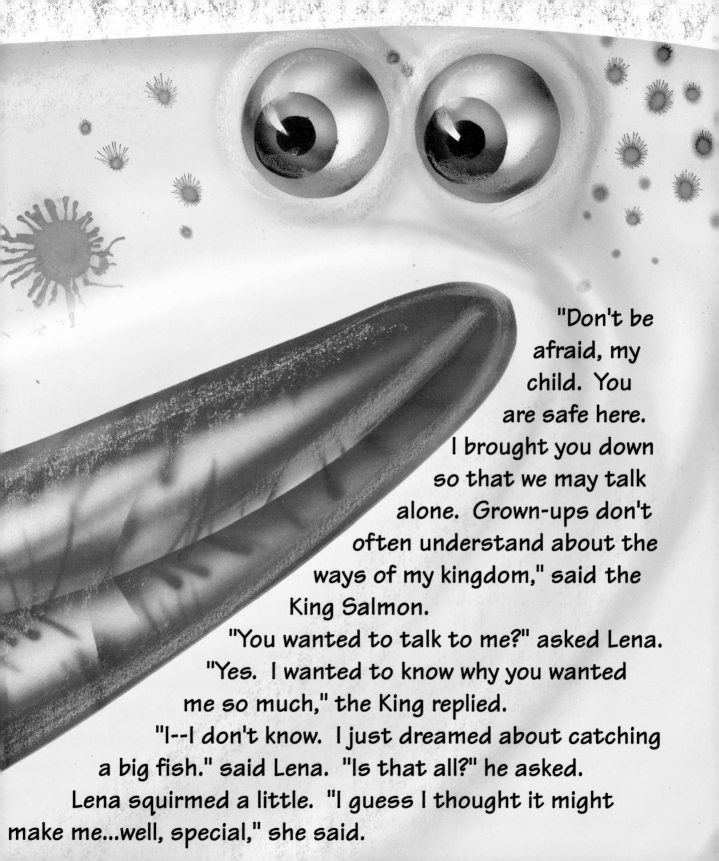

"Don't be
afraid, my
child. You
are safe here.
I brought you down
so that we may talk
alone. Grown-ups don't
often understand about the
ways of my kingdom," said the
King Salmon.
"You wanted to talk to me?" asked Lena.
"Yes. I wanted to know why you wanted
me so much," the King replied.
"I--I don't know. I just dreamed about catching
a big fish." said Lena. "Is that all?" he asked.
Lena squirmed a little. "I guess I thought it might
make me...well, special," she said.

"Hmm...," said the King Salmon. "Come swim with me in the kingdom, Lena. Look around. Tell me what you see."

It felt wonderful to swim beside the big fish and feel the water rushing past. At first Lena couldn't see anything, but as she grew used to the glacial blue river, she began to see amazing things.

"Look over there," she cried. "It's a dancing fish. Why, fish don't dance!"

"Oh, is that so?" said the King Salmon. "But that fish believes she can. So please don't tell her. She loves to dance."

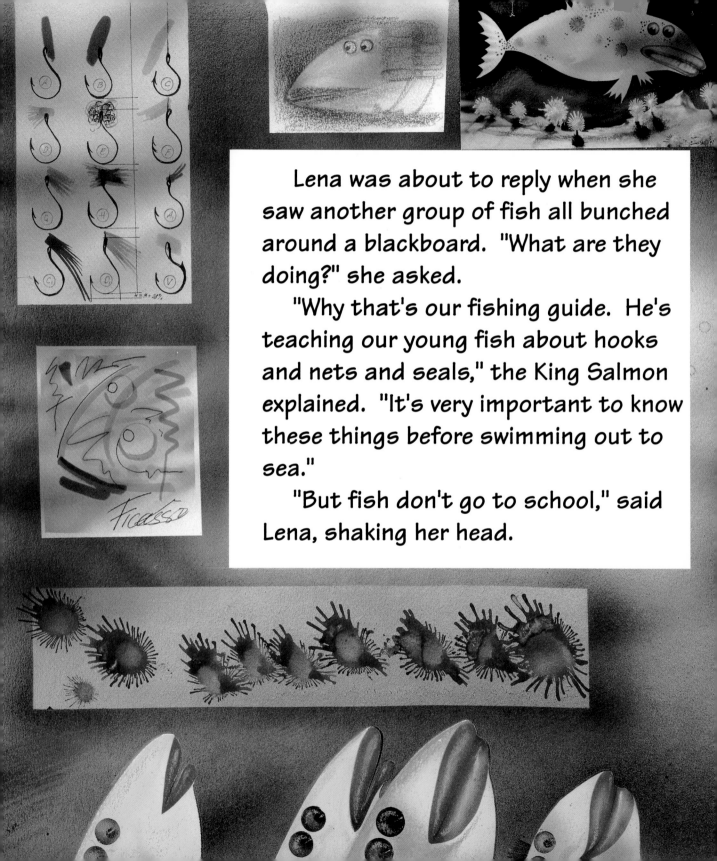

Lena was about to reply when she saw another group of fish all bunched around a blackboard. "What are they doing?" she asked.

"Why that's our fishing guide. He's teaching our young fish about hooks and nets and seals," the King Salmon explained. "It's very important to know these things before swimming out to sea."

"But fish don't go to school," said Lena, shaking her head.

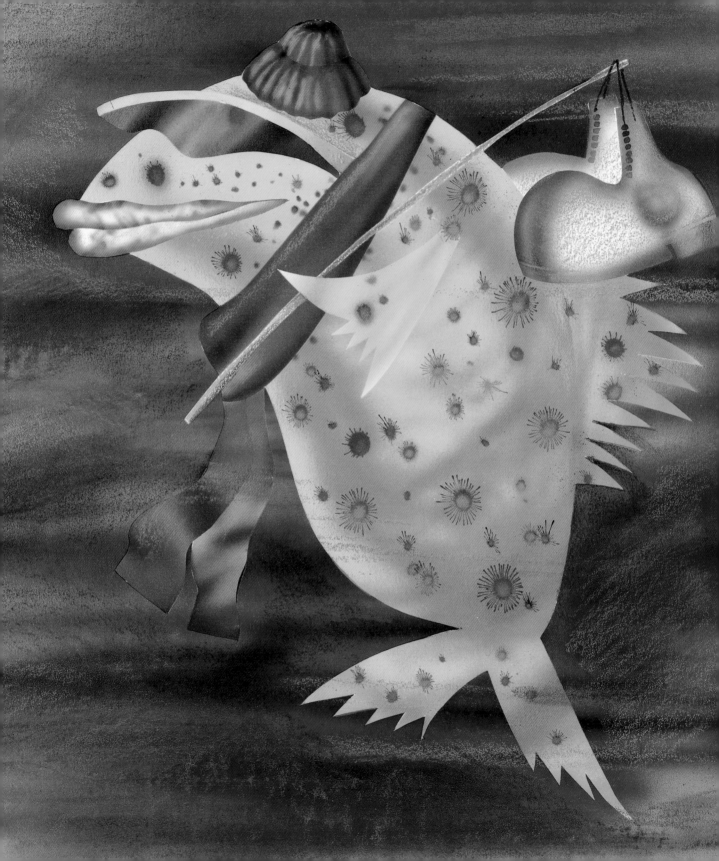

"Oh is that so?" said the King Salmon. "But those fish believe they can. So please don't tell them. We want them to return someday."

Lena was about to say more when she noticed another fish dressed warmly and packed for a long journey.

"Who's that?" asked Lena.

"Oh, that's our famous explorer. He's off to try and reach the North Pole," explained King Salmon.

"But fish don't--" began Lena and then she stopped.

The fish looked at her kindly and smiled.

"I know," said Lena. "He looks like he really loves exploring."

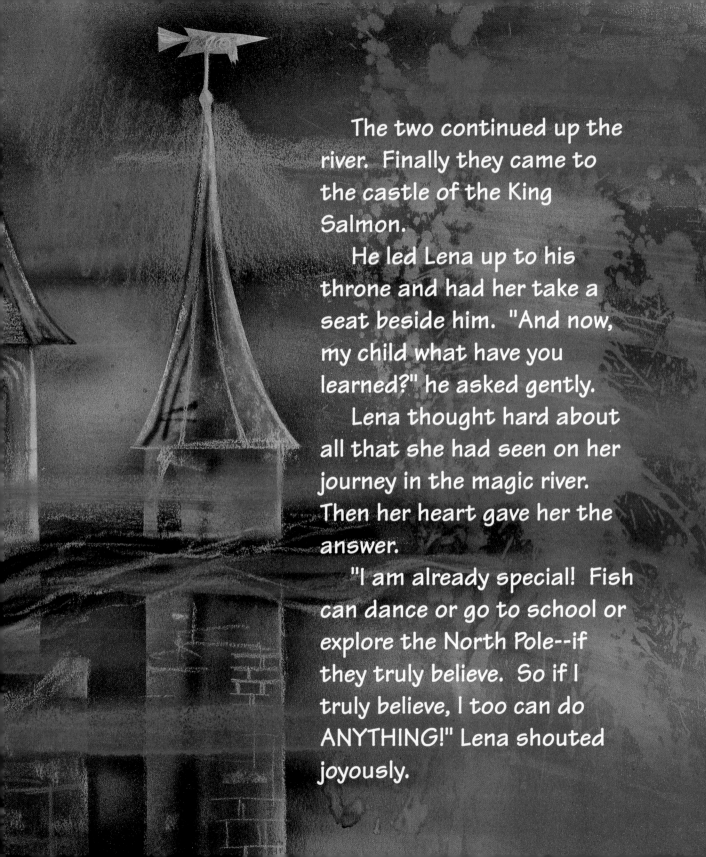

The two continued up the river. Finally they came to the castle of the King Salmon.

He led Lena up to his throne and had her take a seat beside him. "And now, my child what have you learned?" he asked gently.

Lena thought hard about all that she had seen on her journey in the magic river. Then her heart gave her the answer.

"I am already special! Fish can dance or go to school or explore the North Pole--if they truly believe. So if I truly believe, I too can do ANYTHING!" Lena shouted joyously.

Then the King Salmon
smiled his biggest smile. And
the magic river began to shimmer
and shine--pink and green and blue and yellow.
Lena felt herself lifted up, up, up on the big fish's back
through the rainbow of color. Then she slid off the big
fish's back onto the soft river bank.

"Good-bye, King Salmon. I hope I'll see you again,"
Lena whispered. As she hugged the wisest woman, her
heart was singing.

So if, my friend, like Lena,
  you feel a little small,
  If you feel you're unimportant,
    or you feel you're nothing at all,
      Remember this story of Lena,
        a magical tale, yet true,
          If you have a dream,
            you can do anything,
              when you believe in
                YOU......

Alexander "Sasha" Sagan, born and raised in Russia, is currently living in Alaska. He has illustrated five children's books in Russia, and his art work has been exhibited internationally. While growing up, Sasha swam with King Salmon. He credits that experience with his knowledge of life under the water.

Marcia Wakeland is a freelance writer who lost her heart to Alaska 18 years ago. She lives with her husband Steve, and two children, Jon and Karrie, in the Chugach Mountains near Eagle River, Alaska. She believes that all children can realize their dreams, and she has a secret desire to swim with a King Salmon.

A special thanks to Alaska Aquarium

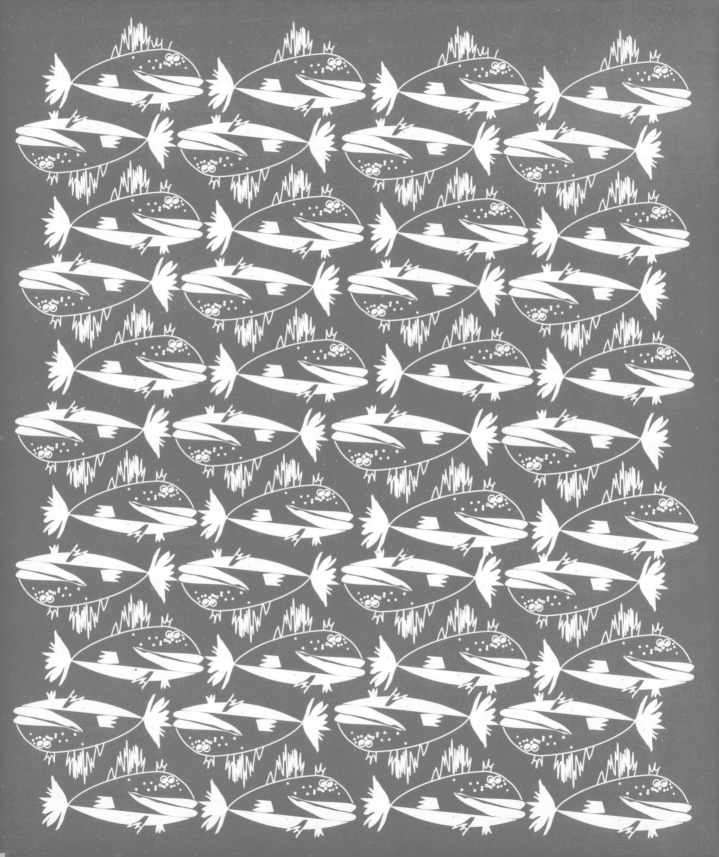